A MASTER MENACE!

BEANObooks

published under licence by

meadowside
CHILDREN'S BOOKS

THE MERRY MENACE

Dennis was bored. He had tried playing football with Gnasher, but the ball had landed in the middle of Mum's freshly baked cake. He had tried teaching Bea to fire a catapult, but she had just hit him on the nose with it and giggled. He had wrapped himself in a sheet and pretended to be a ghost, but Mum hadn't even batted an eyelid.

"I've seen it all before, Dennis," she said.

"HUMPH!" said Dennis. "I've got to get some new menaces."

Dennis and Gnasher mooched and grumped around the house all morning. Finally they slumped down on the sofa where Mum was reading 'Robin Hood' to Bea. It was Bea's favourite story. She loved hearing about how Robin Hood made Friar Tuck carry him across the river. She enjoyed the fight he had with Little John. It made her giggle to hear about him shooting arrows and ambushing rich men in Sherwood Forest. But Dennis was not impressed. He had always much preferred the Sheriff of Nottingham.

"What a load of rubbish," he grumbled. "I can understand the 'taking from the rich part', but I'm not so sure about the 'giving to the poor'."

Suddenly he had a brilliant idea. He quickly scribbled a couple of notes and tucked them under Gnasher's collar. Then he whispered in the Tripe Hound's ear. Gnasher barked and dashed off, as fast as he could, to deliver them.

"He's better than a postman!" Dennis grinned. He grabbed his boots and headed for the door, looking excited. Mum followed him into the hall.

"Where are you going?" she asked in a worried voice. She always felt a bit worried when Dennis looked so excited.

"I'm going to play Robin Hood in

the woods," Dennis told her. "Great story, Mum." He put on his most innocent expression.

Normally Mum would have been very suspicious about this but, just then, Bea started to wail. Mum forgot about Dennis's game and rushed to see what was wrong.

"Thanks, little sis'!" chuckled Dennis and he headed out for the woods.

Curly and Pie Face were waiting by the big oak tree with Gnasher, looking puzzled.

"What's going on?" asked Curly. "What did your note mean?"

"Did you bring what I told you?" Dennis asked. Curly held out three toy bows and twenty arrows with little suckers on the ends.

"But what are they for?" asked Pie Face.

"Ever heard how Robin Hood took from the rich and gave to the poor?" asked Dennis.

"Yeah, of course," said Pie Face and Curly together.

"Well, everyone comes through the wood on the way back from the supermarket. We're gonna collect some taxes – 'cause poor menaces like us need a feast!"

They made a hiding place behind an oak tree. The squirrels and birds that lived in the tree all left quickly. They had seen Dennis before, and they knew it was a good idea to keep out of his way. Gnasher chased a few rabbits out of the undergrowth. Everything was ready.

"What now?" asked Pie Face.

"Now we wait," said Dennis, squatting behind the oak tree.

They didn't have to wait long. Soon they heard footsteps crunching on the path through the woods. It was Minnie and she was carrying a heavy-looking bag.

They waited until she was under the oak tree then Dennis, Pie Face and Curly jumped out in front of her with their bows and arrows.

"Aha, Maid Minnie," said Dennis. "I am Dennis Hood,

8

and these are my merry men and dog. Now, what's in the bag? We need taxes!"

Minnie opened the bag. It was full of sweets, bags of crisps and comics.

"Passage through the woods will cost you three bags of crisps," said Dennis.

Minnie handed him the crisps, seething. "I'll get you for this, Dennis," she snapped.

"Report me to the Sheriff of Nottingham," grinned Dennis, as Minnie stomped away.

Curly and Pie Face sniggered. Then Dennis put his finger to his lips and beckoned to them.

"Shh!" he whispered. **"Listen!"**

Curly and Pie Face listened hard. Very, very faintly they could hear voices. It sounded like singing. The terrible sound grew louder and louder, and soon they could hear the words.

"If you go down to the woods today, you're sure of a big surprise!"

(sang a weedy voice.)

"If you go down to the woods today, you'd better go in disguise!"

(warbled an even weedier voice.)

"For every bear that ever there was Will gather there for certain because—"

(trilled a third.)

"Today's the day the teddy bears have their picnic!"

(sang all the voices together.)

Dennis stuck his fingers in his ears.

"Ugh," he grimaced. "I know those softy voices. Time for a n o t h e r ambush!"

Down the path skipped Walter, Bertie Blenkinsop and Spotty Perkins. They were carrying a picnic basket, a checked blanket and dozens of teddy bears.

"Hold it!" cried Dennis, pointing his bow and arrow at them. "We are the outlaws of Beanotown Forest and you have to pay a softy tax to get through the wood!"

"Go away Dennis," sneered Walter. "We're going to have a teddy bears' picnic."

"Fine," grinned Dennis. "It will cost you three sausage rolls and three sandwiches!"

"No way!" said Walter, folding his puny arms.

"Then you will have to face a challenge!" said Dennis. "Robin Hood was pretty good with a bow and arrow, but nobody's better than me with a catapult! I challenge you to a catapult competition!"

"Ooo! Catapults are r-rather d-dangerous!"

trembled Walter. "I might hurt my delicate fingers!"

"What are you gonna fire?" asked Pie Face.

Dennis and Curly lifted the lid of the picnic basket and peered inside.

"Perfect," grinned Curly. "Squashy tomatoes!"

Pie Face drew a target circle on the oak tree and Dennis took aim with his best catapulting arm. POW!

"Bullseye!" yelled Dennis. "Now it's your turn, Walter. If you can hit a bullseye, I'll let you off the softy tax!"

Walter held up the catapult, closed his eyes in terror, and pulled.

"**OW!**" yelled Spotty as the squashy tomato hit him SLAP in the face.

"Sorry!" squeaked Walter. The three outlaws roared with laughter.

"That's entertainment!" Dennis guffawed. "You can pass through the woods – no tax required!"

Walter narrowed his eyes and glared at him.

"You'll be sorry for this, Dennis!"

"Report me to the Sheriff of Nottingham!" Dennis chuckled as the softies picked up their picnic basket and went along the path. The outlaws settled down to wait for the next visitor.

Soon Sergeant Slipper came strolling down the path. He gave a shout of surprise when the three menaces jumped out in front of him, brandishing bows and arrows.

"Aha, the Sheriff of Beanotown himself!" exclaimed Dennis. "I am Dennis Hood and I demand taxes!"

"Clear off!" bellowed Sergeant Slipper.

"I know you always keep packets of sweets in your helmet for emergencies," said Dennis.

16

"We tax you two packets!"

Sergeant Slipper held onto his helmet with both hands. "Or what?" he asked nastily.

"Fire!" yelled Dennis. Three arrows flew at Sergeant Slipper and stuck to his helmet like porcupine quills. The outlaws put new arrows in their bows.

"All right!" blazed Sergeant Slipper. He took his helmet off and handed over two packets of Chewy Chuckles. "You'll be sorry for this!"

He stormed off through the wood, while the outlaws fell about laughing behind him.

The next person to come marching along the path was the Colonel. He had a fat newspaper under his arm and he was singing an old war song.

"Tum Tum Tarahh!" he warbled. Dennis and Curly jumped out from behind the bush as Pie Face covered his ears.

"Halt!" Dennis cried. "The outlaws of Beanotown Forest demand a tax to walk through the wood!"

"Outrageous!" burbled the Colonel. Dennis saw the fat newspaper fall from under his arm and he sniggered.

"The tax will be two comics!" he announced.

"Hurrumph! I don't have any comics!" blustered the irate Colonel. "I only read serious newspapers!"

"What are those then?" asked Dennis, pointing at the newspaper that had fallen open on the ground. Inside it were ten comics! The Colonel went bright red.

"Blasted impudence!" he said as he handed over two of the comics.

"Go and tell it to the Sheriff of Nottingham," grinned Curly.

"I will!" roared the Colonel, and he charged off down the path.

"I reckon it's been a good morning's menacing," Dennis said, looking at the sweets and comics. "Let's go back to my house and have an outlaws' feast!"

They tramped back through the wood and along the street to Dennis' house. But when they sneaked in through the back door, they got a shock. Mum was waiting for them. Her arms were folded across her chest and she had a look on her face that Dennis didn't like at all.

"Uh oh!" he said. "Quick, let's get outta here."

They turned to leave, but Dad was there, blocking the doorway and glowering.

"I hear you've been playing Robin Hood," said Dad.

"Er, yeah," admitted Dennis.

"Yes, we've heard all about your little game," added Mum. "We've had lots of visitors – Minnie, Walter, the Colonel, Sergeant Slipper ..."

"Well—" began Pie Face.

"They were all telling us how realistic your game was," continued Mum in her most sarcastic voice. "So I thought I'd help you out."

"Eh?" exclaimed Dennis, raising his eyebrows.

"I know you've done the 'taking from the rich' part, but you must have forgotten about 'giving to the poor'," Mum said. "I suppose this must be everything?"

She grabbed the comics and sweets before Dennis could stop her.

"Well well, you have been busy," she added. "How very generous of you, Dennis."

"B-U-T..."

"Don't worry," grinned Dad as the doorbell rang. "It'll all go to a very good cause."

"That'll be the lady from the 'Help the Softies Campaign'," said Mum. "I rang her to say we had lots of things for the softies, and she said she'd come straight away."

She hurried out with the sweets and comics. Dennis gave a howl.

"Now then," said Dad, grabbing
Dennis by the back of his jumper.

"Let's carry on with the game. I'll be the Sheriff of Nottingham, which means I'm in charge. And I seem to remember that the Sheriff wasn't a very nice man. He liked giving orders and making other people work for him."

"Nooo!" moaned Dennis, as Dad pulled a very very long list out of his pocket and pushed all three of them into the garden.

"I've got a whole list of chores for you – cleaning the drains, polishing the car, washing the windows ... and you can start by planting the trees I bought at the garden centre last week, since you seem so interested in forests all of a sudden."

"This isn't how the story ends!" Dennis fumed, clenching his fists.

"It is when I'm telling it!" growled Dad, handing each of them a spade.

"NOW GET DIGGING!"

"The perfect ending," chuckled Mum as the three menaces puffed and panted. "They don't look so merry now!"

RECORD BREAKER

Everyone was talking about it. There were posters on every wall. There were leaflets through every letterbox.

Record Breakers was coming to Beanotown.

"Anyone can try to break a record," Dennis told Gnasher at breakfast. "It can be anything at all."

"It's a very exciting day for Beanotown," said Dad, waving his fork in the air.

Gnasher snaffled Dad's sausages while he was looking at the leaflet.

28

He wondered if there was a record for the number of sausages eaten in one minute.

"I'm gonna do the highest-ever skateboarding jump," Dennis went on. Gnasher didn't hear him. He was still thinking about the sausages.

"I'm going to bake the largest cake in the world," said Mum.

"You never bake cakes for me," Dad complained.

"There's a reason for that," replied Mum, glancing at Dad's bulging belly.

"The chaps at the golf club are going for the longest game of golf ever," said Dad.

"Also known as 'how to bore people to death'," Dennis added.

"Well, we'll just see who ends up in the Big Book of Records, won't we?" Dad replied. "It's about time this family did something to be proud of. Even Bea is going to try for a record."

"What, how many stinky nappies she can get through in one day?" asked Dennis, grimacing at his little sister.

"Don't be such a pest, Dennis,"
said Mum. "Bea is going to make
the biggest ever hand painting with
the playgroup."

Dennis stuffed the last piece of
toast into his mouth and stood up.

"Ahmoooppffgmm,"

he said, spraying toast
crumbs over the table.

"Manners, young man!"
roared Dad.

"I'm going to practise my
skateboarding jumps," Dennis
said, gulping the toast down.
"See you later!"

"That boy is too much of a
menace to win any records,"
grumbled Dad, shaking toast
crumbs out of his moustache.

Dennis and Gnasher whizzed through town on the skateboard. Walter was standing in front of the Record Breakers poster with Foo-Foo, reading the rules.

"Are you going for the 'biggest softy in Beanotown' record?" Dennis shouted as he sped past.

Walter stuck out his tongue.

"I'd rather be a softy than a menace!" he shouted.

"You're mad!" guffawed Dennis. But when they reached the skatepark, it was locked up. There was a big sign on the gate:

CLOSED

FOR REPAIRS
NO ENTRY TO ANYONE
(ESPECIALLY DENNIS)

Dennis looked over the fence to see if he could get in, but there were diggers all over the park. The skateboarding ramps were in pieces. The whole park was being dug up.

"Rats," scowled Dennis. "Now I'll have to think of somewhere else to practise."

Just then Curly came whizzing around the corner on his skateboard.

"Aha, just what I need, a menacing helper," grinned Dennis. "Come on, Curly mate, we're going to have some fun."

Gnasher gave a growly, sausagey sort of bark.

"No worries, Gnasher," added Dennis. "If you want sausages, I know just the place."

They boarded back into town and slowed down as they came to the butcher's. Gnasher grabbed all the strings of sausages hanging up outside the shop, then Dennis put on a spurt of speed as the butcher ran after them, shaking his fist.

"Bloomin' menace!"

they heard him yell as they made their getaway.

"So where are we gonna practise?" asked Curly. "The park's in pieces."

"You have to trust the best menacing mind in the country," said Dennis, tapping his head.

First they went to Curly's house.

"Got anything we can jump off?" asked Dennis. Curly looked around the garden. His eyes came to rest on his dad's shed.

"Wahoooooooo-0-0-0!"

cried Dennis a few minutes later, as he hurtled down the sloping shed roof and looped through the air, before landing in the vegetable patch. "Three sixty!" Marrows and lettuces flew into the air.

"Brilliant!" cried Curly. "Now it's my turn!"

But just then there was a loud creeeaaakk. With a groan of timber, the shed roof collapsed. All four walls fell outwards. The only thing left standing was Curly's dad's lawnmower. There was a yell of hysterical fury from the sitting room window. Curly's dad stood there, purple in the face.

"Scarper!" shouted Curly, jumping onto his skateboard. Dennis and Gnasher were close behind. They rumbled down the pavement at top speed. Soft boy Bertie Blenkinsop was ahead of them, singing as he skipped along.

"Next stop the Colonel's!" called Dennis, swerving to make sure he hit Bertie. The Colonel had a training ground in his back garden. The best part of it was a high, curving wall for his toy soldiers to climb.

"Drop-in!" grinned Dennis. He and Curly balanced on the top of the curving wall.

Dennis shot down the curve, did a perfect aciddrop move and landed in the Colonel's goldfish pond.

Curly followed him down the curve, kickflipped and landed next to Dennis with a loud splash.

"Getting higher," grinned Dennis, shaking a goldfish out of his jumper. "Shall we do it again?"

"Er, I think we'd better practise our top speed," stammered Curly, pointing. The Colonel was stamping down the path towards them. His face was going scarlet.

"Hold him off, Gnasher!" yelled Dennis, as he and Curly pulled out their skateboards from the pond. Gnasher snarled and grabbed the Colonel's trouser legs in his jaws.

"Company dismissed!" laughed Dennis as they escaped.

"Where next?" asked Curly. "There's no point going to your house. The Colonel, the butcher and my dad will all be waiting for us there."

"Let's head to the woods," said Dennis. "There's a brilliant place to practise there."

When they reached the woods, they picked their way through the hanging branches.

"We're almost there," said Dennis. "I'll show you my latest trick – a sausagegrind. You'll love this one, Gnasher."

But Gnasher was pricking up his ears and growling. Dennis and Curly listened too. They could hear very faint singing...

"Round and round the garden,
                    like a teddy bear..."

"I know that weedy voice!" said Dennis with a menacing grin. "But what's he doing in the woods? I thought he was scared of the squirrels!"

Dennis and Curly tiptoed towards the singing. They saw Walter, Bertie and Spotty sitting in a little clearing. Around them were piles and piles of picked daisies.

"My skateboarding practise spot!" growled Dennis. He jumped onto his board and whizzed into the clearing. Curly followed him and they wheeled round and round the three softies.

"What are you doing here?" roared Dennis. "I need to practise my skateboarding moves!"

"You're not doing that stupid sport here!"

said Walter pompously. "We're making the longest daisy chain in the world, so leave us alone, Dennis. You haven't got the brains to understand."

42

"Oh yeah? Well I'm going in for a record too – a skateboarding record. Shall we tell them all about it, Curly? See, the first thing you learn in boarding is how to do an ollie..."

Dennis jumped into the air with his board and landed on top of the pile of daisies, squashing them.

"My daisies!" yelled Spotty.

"Then of course there's the kickflip..." Curly flipped his board and kicked Bertie's bottom...

"and the kickturn..." Dennis booted Spotty's backside.

"Nothing to it," shrugged Dennis, sticking his board under his arm.

Walter picked up the rest of his daisies and glared at Dennis.

"You'll be sorry for this, you menace!"

Walter stormed off, closely followed by Bertie and Spotty.

Curly and Dennis practised some more moves and Dennis did some very high jumps. By the time he headed home, he was sure that he was in with a chance for a record. But when he got to the house, Dad grabbed his skateboard from under his arm.

"**Oi!**" bellowed Dennis.

"This is going to be locked away," roared Dad. "Walter has told me that you crushed all his daisies!"

"That cry-baby, tell-tale, sneaking softy!"

steamed Dennis. "I didn't crush all his daisies! He was in my practise area! You can't take my board away – the judges are coming this afternoon!"

"Tough luck,"

said Dad, going to lock the board away in his shed.

Dennis stomped out to the garden. All the neighbours were outside, practising for their record attempts.

45

Sergeant Slipper rode past on a unicycle. Dennis's eyes narrowed.

"If I can't get a record," he said to Gnasher, "no one's gonna get a record."

He pulled out his catapult and aimed. TWANG! He hit the spokes of the unicycle and Sergeant Slipper fell forward, landing on his head. His head got wedged so far inside his helmet that he couldn't see anything. He blundered around with his arms stretched out in front of him. Dennis sniggered.

He was standing just underneath the kitchen window and he could hear Mum talking to Bea.

"I've finished the cake," she said. "It's got twenty-five layers – that must be a record! Time for your nap, Bea. Come on."

A funny sort of smile spread over Dennis's face. He heard Mum take Bea upstairs, then he and Gnasher sneaked into the kitchen. The cake was on the table. It was so high that it almost touched the ceiling. It was a chocolate cake, crammed full of strawberries and raspberries.

"Right Gnasher," Dennis said. **"Tuck in!"**

Ten minutes later, there was nothing left of the record-breaking cake but a few chocolatey crumbs. Dennis gave a loud burp and a big sigh of pleasure. Gnasher was lying on his side, panting loudly. Both of them were covered in chocolate.

"That's two record breakers dealt with," said Dennis. "Now for Dad."

It took Dennis and Gnasher quite a long time to walk to Dad's golf club. They were very full of cake and they could only walk very slowly. But at last they reached the green. Dad was chatting to some other golfers. They were all wearing diamond-patterned jumpers and ridiculous hats. And none of them was watching their golf clubs.

Within minutes, Dennis had all the golf clubs tucked under his arms. He marched off and buried them in a large bunker.

"They'll never think to look for them there," he told Gnasher. "Now I need Bea's menacing help."

When he reached Bea's nursery, the great record-breaking painting had already started. All the infants were outside, using tubs of paint to decorate an enormous piece of paper with hand and foot prints. Bea was not joining in. She had her arms folded and a big frown on her face. This was not her idea of fun.

Dennis called his little sister over and whispered in her ear. A big smile spread across her face.

Just then Dennis saw the judges heading for Bea's school.

"Quick!" he told her.

Bea crawled over to the paint pots and started to push. One by one she pushed them all to where Dennis was hiding. He pulled some balloons from his back pocket and started to fill them with paint. Then Bea dragged the big piece of paper over to him. He quickly made it into an enormous paper plane.

"Well done," whispered Dennis. "You're going to make a great menace. Now, you're little enough to fly this thing. You know what you've gotta do!"

Bea jumped into the paper plane and Dennis put the balloons into her lap. Then he picked up the plane and launched it into the air with all his strength. Bea flew over the heads of the teachers and splattered them with her colourful paint bombs.

The teachers ran around and around, trying to get away from Bea's paint bomber. Dennis roared with laughter. The infants giggled and cheered as their teachers were soaked in bright colours. Then the paper plane started to land.

Dennis turned and started to run. Suddenly he heard someone calling his name.

"Dennis, STOP!"

He turned around. The judges were walking up to the nursery and beckoning to him.

"Come here!" they called. They were smiling.

Dennis walked up to them, ready to run if things turned nasty. The first judge was a young man in a boarding t-shirt and combat trousers. The second judge was a young woman with spiky pink hair and a ring through her nose.

"Are you Dennis?" asked the first judge.

"Errrrrm, what if I am?" asked Dennis suspiciously.

"We've been looking for you everywhere! I'm Raf and this is Kim. We've been trying to judge the record breaking, but it's impossible. You get there first every time."

"Yeah, well—" began Dennis.

"The cake," said Raf.

"The golf clubs," added Kim.

"The daisy chain," they both laughed.

"There's nothing left to judge," said Raf. "So there's only one record breaker in Beanotown."

"Who?" blazed Dennis. "Who did I miss out?"

"Dennis," said Kim, pulling out a medal, "this is for you. You are officially the World's Number One Menace!"

SERGEANT SLIPPER

Curly and Pie Face came to Dennis's house early on a bright Saturday morning.

"Ready?" they called to Dennis.

"Where are you going?" asked Mum. "Why are you up so early?"

"Fishing," said Dennis, waving his fishing rod. Mum relaxed.

"That sounds nice and normal," she said hopefully. "Make sure you catch something – we can have it for tea!" The three menaces strolled down the road with their fishing rods over their shoulders. They walked down the riverside path that led into town. A footbridge arched over the path. As they walked towards the bridge, Dennis elbowed Curly and Pie Face in the ribs.

"Ow!" Curly complained.

"Oof!" groaned Pie Face.

"Look!" Dennis pointed.

A fisherman was sitting by the river, under a huge green umbrella. He was wearing a green wax jacket, a big hat and long wellies. Dennis, Curly and Pie Face stopped next to him. He looked really grumpy.

"Have you caught anything?" Dennis asked.

"Shut up!" hissed the man. "You'll scare the fish off."

"Do you think it's going to rain?"
asked Curly, puzzled. He looked at
the umbrella, then up at the blue sky.
"Buzz off!" said the man.

"Bit chilly are you?" added Pie Face, looking at the thick jacket. "Summer not hot enough for you?"

"Clear off, you stupid pests," snapped the fisherman, turning around to glare at them. "And you'd better not be planning to use those rods here! This is my patch!"

Dennis raised his eyebrows. "Come on, lads," he said. "If we can't do any proper fishing, we'll have to think of something else!" And he winked menacingly.

They clambered up onto the footbridge over the path. Then they sat down on the edge.

"Only idiots go fishing for fish," said Dennis loudly.

"Yeah," said Curly. "You would have thought someone would have told him about supermarkets!

The fisherman turned again and shook his fist at them.

They dangled their fishing lines off the edge of the bridge, but not over the river. All three lines hung over the footpath. The fisherman shook his head.

"Mad,"

he muttered crossly under his breath. Dennis, Pie Face and Curly waved at him cheerfully.

Soon they saw someone walking towards them along the path.

"It's the Colonel," said Dennis. "Excellent. You know, it's pretty hot today. I don't think he needs that heavy hat…"

The boys dangled their rods carefully as the Colonel marched along the path. Dennis and Pie Face missed, but Curly's hook slipped under the brim and lifted the hat neatly into the air.

"Quick!" hissed Dennis, as the Colonel looked wildly around him. They pulled the hat up and hid their rods behind their backs. The Colonel looked up and saw them. He started to puff up like a balloon.

"You!" he barked. "What have you done with my hat?"

"The wind must have blown it off," said Dennis innocently.

"There's no wind at all, boy! You grabbed it off my head!"

"How could I do a thing like that from all the way up here?" Dennis exclaimed, opening his eyes very wide. "My arms would have to be ten feet long!"

"Hurrrumph!" said the Colonel, but he couldn't argue with that.

"Will you shut UP!" bellowed the fisherman, turning to glare at the Colonel.

"Insolence in the ranks!" the Colonel roared. He stomped off in the direction of town, muttering about having to buy a new hat. Dennis chuckled and put the hat on Curly's head.

"Your first catch of the day!" he said. "And here comes another one – look!"

Walter was skipping along the path, stopping every few seconds to pick flowers. "You know," Dennis said, "Walter picks way too many flowers. It's not good for the environment. But he can't pick 'em … if he can't see 'em …"

Dennis gave his fishing rod a flick. The hook flew through the air and snatched Walter's glasses – they were in Dennis' hand before Walter knew what had happened.

"HELP!" he shouted, stumbling around blindly. "Where did my glasses go?"

The fisherman turned around in a fury.

"I'm sick of you blinkin' kids!" he hissed. "I haven't caught a single fish yet!

CLEAR OFF!"

"Yes sir, sorry sir," said Walter. He squinted his eyes up and walked slowly on towards town. "Mumsy will just have to buy me a new pair," he whined as he went under the bridge.

Dennis put the glasses in his back pocket.

The next person to come strolling down the path was Dennis's dad. He was heading towards the golf club with his newspaper tucked under his arm.

"Dad never reads the paper," grinned Dennis. "He just goes to sleep behind it."

"Go for it, Pie Face," said Curly. Pie Face stuck his tongue out to help him concentrate and cast his line. It snaked over Dad's shoulder and neatly hooked the paper.

"Brilliant shot!" said Dennis.

'HIDE IT QUICK!"

Dad spun around, thinking there was someone behind him. Pie Face hid the rod and the paper behind his back. Dad looked up and saw them all grinning . His moustache bristled.

Where's my paper?" he bellowed. "Dennis, hand it over!"

Dennis held out his hands. "How could I have taken your paper, Dad? I can't reach that far!"

"Well where's it gone, then?"

"Maybe the wind blew it away."

"Oh yes, the wind loves a good read," said Dad, sarcastically. "If I find out you're behind this…"

He shook his finger at the three lads and carried on into town. Pie Face pulled out the newspaper and swatted Curly on the head with it.

"We've caught three!" Dennis yelled down to the grumpy fisherman. "How about you?"

"SHUT UP!"

roared the fisherman, so loud that it made his own head ring.

"Shhh," said Dennis, shaking his head sadly. "You'll scare the fish."

"Argghh!" the fisherman yelled. He pulled off his hat and stamped on it.

"Temper temper," scolded Dennis.

"There's no point in staying here now. All the fish will be ten miles away!"

The fisherman packed up his gear and glared up at the grinning menaces.

"You pests are going to be sorry," he growled. "Just you wait and see."

"You'll be waiting a long time," said Dennis. The fisherman gave a final snort of disgust and headed into town.

"Good riddance," said Curly. "Who'll be next?"

No one came along the path for a long time. Dennis started to get bored. Then he saw Sergeant Slipper, plodding slowly away from the town towards them.

"Best yet," grinned Dennis. "Get ready, lads!"

They all cast their lines and Dennis snagged the policeman's helmet. It flew through the air and landed in his lap. Sergeant Slipper turned around, very slowly. Then, to their surprise, he looked straight at them. He had a horrible, smug expression on his face.

"Oho," he said. "Knocking a policeman's helmet off is a crime, you know."

"Us?
Knock your helmet off?"

gasped Dennis. "How could we do that from all the way up here?"

"Your little game's over," smirked Sergeant Slipper.

Suddenly they felt their fishing rods yanked out of their hands. The bad-tempered fisherman was standing right behind them!

"I told you," he called down to Sergeant Slipper.

"They're a nasty, rotten pack of troublemakers," agreed Sergeant Slipper. He walked up the bank to the bridge and took the fishing rods.

"These are being confiscated," he said. "And I'll have my helmet back as well."

The fisherman gave Dennis a nasty grin, then walked off with Sergeant Slipper. Dennis scowled and reached into his pocket. He pulled out a piece of sticky paper, scribbled 'Kick Me!' on it. Then he very quickly stuck it on Sergeant Slipper's broad back without him noticing anything at all.

"It's not much of a menace," he told Curly and Pie Face with a shrug, "but it'll do for now. Come on!"

They followed Sergeant Slipper at a distance. The fisherman waved goodbye to him and Sergeant Slipper plodded down the High Street. Everyone he passed noticed the sticker on his back. They started to laugh and point. Sergeant Slipper couldn't understand it. He checked his tunic for egg stains. He checked his trouser legs for small dogs. There was nothing there. Then one little boy twitched his foot, stepped backwards, took careful aim and

THWACK!

He kicked Sergeant Slipper's oversized bottom.

"Oi you!" yelled Sergeant Slipper. "What do you think you're playing at?"

"You can't blame the kid," Pie Face called. "Your sticker told him to do it!"

Sergeant Slipper reached round with a lot of huffing and puffing and pulled the sticker off his back. When he read it he went even redder than before.

"You pack of menaces!" he bellowed. "I'll have you behind bars for this!"

"You'll have to catch us first!" retorted Dennis. And the great Beanotown chase began.

Sergeant Slipper chased them through streets and alleyways. They dodged round phone boxes and benches, behind fat shoppers and under thin ones. They leapfrogged over small children and used softies as shields.

"Getaway car!" yelled Curly. He saw his grandma's pavement scooter outside a shop. The three boys leapt on it and powered down the street.

"Come back here!" puffed Sergeant Slipper, clutching his sides and panting. The boys cranked the scooter up to top speed. Curly, Pie Face and Dennis clung to the scooter, Gnasher hanging onto the back by his teeth. They sped to the end of the High Street and down the main road towards the zoo.

79

"Look out!" yelled Curly. He pointed – the wall of Beanotown Zoo was straight ahead of them.

"We're gonna crash!" cried Pie Face, in a panic. Gnasher put his paws over his eyes. But Dennis steered the scooter violently to the left and they shot through the open door of the staff entrance.

Dennis hit the brakes. The scooter shuddered to a halt in front of the elephant enclosure. There was a big sign saying 'Ella the Elephant, and underneath it was Ella herself. She looked very bored.

"The zoo's not open yet," said Curly, looking around.

"We can hide from Sergeant Slipper in here," Pie Face added.

"Time for a bit of fun, you mean," said Dennis.

The Zoo Keeper was inside the elephant enclosure, cleaning it out and grumbling to himself. He had left all his buckets of water by the wall. Dennis jerked his thumb at them and winked. The boys crept over and picked up a bucket each. Ella stuck her trunk over the top of her enclosure wall. Dennis, Pie Face and Curly tiptoed over to the waving trunk. They held up the buckets and Ella slurped the water into her trunk – one … two … three bucketfuls. Then she turned slowly around and aimed her trunk at the zookeeper.

POW!

A jet of water hit him right in the backside!

Ella gave a loud trumpet.

"**Strike!**" yelled the boys.

"You menaces!" spluttered the zookeeper.

"Run!" shouted Pie Face. They ran further into the zoo and stopped by the monkey cage. There was a big bowl of bananas next to it, waiting for feeding time. The zookeeper was close behind them. Dennis grabbed a handful of bananas and chucked them at the zookeeper. He dodged and jumped, but finally he slipped and landed **SPLAT** on a banana.

Before he could get to his feet again, Dennis, Curly and Pie Face ran back through the zoo to where they had left the scooter. The zookeeper did not seem to be following them any more. They jumped back on the scooter and raced out of the zoo and up the high street.

"Keep a lookout for Slipper!" ordered Dennis as he steered around the first corner. But suddenly he didn't seem to be going anywhere. He pressed the accelerator but the scooter wouldn't move.

"Never mind Slipper!" yelled Curly, "Grandma Alert!"

They all looked over their shoulders. Curly's grandma had hooked her walking stick over the back of the scooter and was tugging on it with all her strength. And she had brought all her friends to help her.

Twenty furious elderly people were hanging on to the scooter with their walking sticks. Dennis turned around again and gave a yell – Sergeant Slipper was standing right in front of them, his arms folded and his face red.

"I've been very busy with complaints this morning," he said.

"Very busy indeed. And I've just had another one from my friend the zookeeper. So I think we'd all better go and see him together."

The little old lady unhooked her cane and used the other end to prod Dennis in the ribs.

"Off my scooter!" she screeched.

"We were only borrowing it," grumbled Dennis, getting off with Curly and Pie Face. "And we're not going back to the zoo."

"Oho, I think you are," smirked Sergeant Slipper. Twenty walking sticks bristled in their direction. They were trapped!

Dennis, Curly, Pie Face and Gnasher were pushed and prodded back down the road to the zoo.

Every time they tried to break away, someone's walking stick would stomp on their feet. At last, limping and complaining, they arrived at the zoo. The zookeeper, who was still covered in squashed bananas, met them at the entrance.

"Aha," he said. "Come with me."

He pushed them into a building and through a low door. They were in a large room with straw on the ground and three walls. But where the fourth wall should have been there were just …

Bars!

They were in the monkey cage!

Sergeant Slipper was outside with the fisherman, Dennis's dad and Curly's grandma. Everyone was laughing.

"There are three buckets in there," said the zookeeper, "and you're not coming out until that monkey cage is sparkling clean!"

"ARRRGH!" roared Dennis.

"That's a sight for sore eyes!" Sergeant Slipper chuckled. "I told you three I'd see you behind bars!"

But no one had noticed Ella the elephant. She was watching everything. Those boys had made her laugh for the first time in ages, and now they were in trouble! She filled her trunk with water, took careful aim and ...

POW! Curly's grandma and her friends went down like ninepins!

SPLASH! Sergent Slipper did a backwards somersault as the jet of water hit him!

SPLUTTER! Dennis's dad was drenched from head to foot!

Dennis, Curly and Pie Face ran out of the monkey cage, laughing and cheering.

"It's lucky that elephants never forget!" chuckled Dennis as they made their getaway.

GNEEK! FOR THE BEST MENACING ON THE NET...

...CHECK OUT

www.beanotown.com

©D.C.THOMSON & CO., LTD., 2005